DR. WANGARI MAATHAI

PLANTS A FOREST

REBEL GiRLS®

Our books are available at special quantity discounts for bulk purchase for sale promotions, premiums, fundraising, and educational needs. For details, write to sales@rebelgirls.co

Editorial Director: Elena Favilli
Art Director: Giulia Flamini
Text: Corinne Purtill
Cover and Illustrations: Eugenia Mello
Cover Lettering: Cesar Yannarella
Graphic design: Annalisa Ventura
Printed in Italy by Graphicom

This is a work of historical fiction. We have tried to be as accurate as possible, but names, characters, businesses, places, events, locales, and incidents may have been changed to suit the needs of the story.

www.rebelgirls.co

First Edition
ISBN 978-1-7333292-1-7

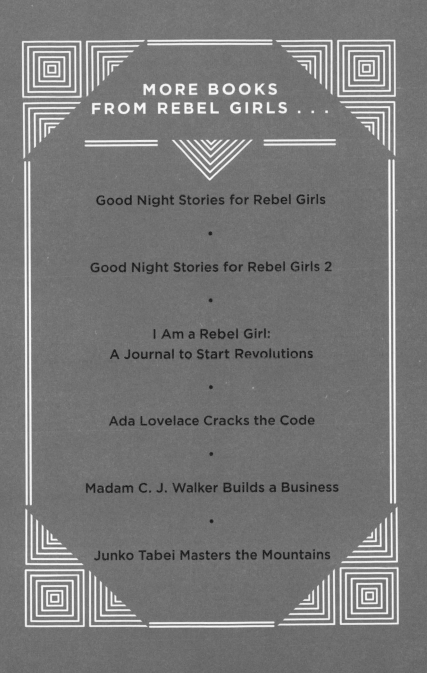

MORE BOOKS
FROM REBEL GIRLS . . .

Good Night Stories for Rebel Girls

•

Good Night Stories for Rebel Girls 2

•

I Am a Rebel Girl:
A Journal to Start Revolutions

•

Ada Lovelace Cracks the Code

•

Madam C. J. Walker Builds a Business

•

Junko Tabei Masters the Mountains

To the Rebel Girls of the world...

Care for your beliefs as
if they were seeds,
then watch them grow.

Dr. Wangari Maathai

April 1, 1940-September 25, 2011

Kenya

I n the central highlands of Kenya, there grew a *mugumo* tree—a tall wild fig with bark as gray and gnarled as an elephant's hide.

Nearby was a stream that bubbled up straight from the earth. And that's where, in 1947, seven-year-old Wangari Muta sat under the enormous leaves of an arrowroot plant and gazed into the waters at the reflection of her favorite tree.

Wangari scooped a delicious drink of cool water to her mouth with her hands. Satisfied, she looked up to where the great mugumo's branches unfurled across the sky. She remembered the first time her mother had brought her here.

"Do you see this tree, Wangari?" her mother

had said, shifting a basket to her hip and smoothing back the bright-red scarf around her hair. "You must never take anything away from it—not even the dry wood for a fire."

"Why, Maitū?"

"The mugumo isn't a tree for people. It's a tree of God. We don't use it. We don't cut it. We don't burn it. They live for as long as they can, and when they are old enough, they fall down on their own."

Wangari had marveled, as she always did, at all the things her mother, Wanjirū, knew about the way the world worked.

Looking back at the bottom of the shallow stream, she saw sparkling beads of black, white, and brown. They were smooth and perfect, just like the beads her grandmother wore. If she could pick them up, she thought maybe she could string them together into a necklace. She reached her hand into the water ever so gently. But as soon as the beads touched her skin, they broke apart.

What happened to them? she wondered, and not for the first time. She'd seen this before and was always surprised. Wangari knew that in a few weeks, the rest of the beads would be gone, too. Instead she'd see tiny tadpoles that would dart from her hands when she tried to catch them. A few days later, she would find the tadpoles missing. Only the occasional frog would hop nearby. It seemed like magic.

She would have to ask her mother about this later. With questions swirling through her mind, Wangari gathered her basket, lifted it onto her back, and started for home.

~

Wangari lived in a village in Kenya called Ihithe. The path from the stream to her house led up a hill through a forest where elephants, antelopes, monkeys, and leopards roamed free. The soil felt sturdy under Wangari's bare feet,

and she kept an eye out for other footprints—and paw prints, too.

"If you are walking on the path and you see the leopard's tail, be careful not to step on it," Maitū had warned her.

But Wangari was not frightened. The word for "leopard" in her language, Kikuyu, was *ngarī*. *Wa-ngarī* meant "belonging to the leopard." If she ever found one, Wangari was sure the beautiful cat would recognize her as one of its own.

As she approached the village, Wangari nodded politely at the women coming from the fields, their woven baskets brimming with roots and greens they'd plucked from the earth. The sun shone on her shoulders as she shouted and waved at other children who, like her, were carrying home their family's firewood and water.

Ahead of her on the dirt path, Wangari could see her mother carrying a basket of vegetables in her arms and her baby brother in a woven sling on her back. Her younger sisters toddled by her mother's skirts.

Her mother was the kindest person Wangari knew. She never yelled or said cross words. At the sight of her family, Wangari broke into a run, being careful not to spill the bouncing basket on her back. Together, they walked the rest of the way home.

"Arrowroots! Thank you, Wangari," her mother said as she set the basket on the lush grass outside their home and handed the baby, Kamunya, to Wangari.

Wangari kissed her brother's chubby cheeks. He giggled and gurgled in return.

This part of the day was Wangari's favorite. She loved when her family gathered around the evening fire, the setting sun throwing golden light over the trees and rooftops. They roasted corn and potatoes, and the smell was wonderful. Ihithe was a village of small houses with mud walls and grass roofs. The Kikuyu, Wangari's people, always built their homes with the doors facing Mount Kenya. It was the place where God lived, Wanjirū had explained to her children. As long as the mountain stood, it was a sign that everything would be all right.

"Tell us a story!" one of her sisters said.

"Yes, Maitū!" Wangari echoed. She sat down with the baby in her lap, and the other children snuggled up next to her.

"All right," her mother said. She picked up one of the knobbly roots and began to shave away the tough bark with her knife.

"One day, a long, long time ago, there was a terrible fire in the forest."

"In our forest, Maitū?" Wangari broke in.

"Not too far from here," her mother said gently. "It was an awful fire, with flames higher than the tallest giraffe. And it was hungry. It moved through the forest eating everything in its path—

the trees, the flowers, everything."

Wangari thought about flames encircling Ihithe, encircling her mugumo tree. She shuddered.

"The animals ran to the highest hill and watched that fire gobbling up their land. The elephant and the leopard, the antelope and the lion: all of them, just standing there. Until someone said, 'We have to do something!' And do you know who that was?"

"Who?" Wangari asked.

"It was the hummingbird. The smallest animal of all. It flew as fast as it could down to the stream. It drank up all the water it could hold in that little mouth"—here Maitū pretended she was drinking, which made Wangari and the other children laugh— "then flew back to that fire and threw all the water onto the flames. It went back to the stream, back to the fire. Over and over again.

"The elephant could hold so much more water in his big nose"—Maitū gave the baby's nose a playful nip, producing a giggle—"but he didn't move. The leopard could run much faster than that little hummingbird, but he didn't move, either."

My *leopard?* Wangari thought.

"At last the antelope cried: 'Little hummingbird, what are you doing?'"

Maitū looked straight at Wangari as she continued, "'I am doing the best I can,' the hummingbird told them. 'I am doing the best I can.'"

The other children begged for another tale, but Wangari was lost in thought. *What good was it to be big like the elephant or powerful like the leopard if you weren't going to help when it mattered?* Maybe she didn't belong only to the leopard. She shared a name with the cat—and a spirit with the hummingbird.

CHAPTER TWO

Wangari knelt in her mother's garden and rubbed her fingers gently over the place where she'd buried a row of beans just the day before. She could hear the nearby *thwack* of her mother's *panga* as it was used to cut through weeds.

Crouching down farther until her nose almost touched the earth, she squinted at the place where she hoped little sprouts would be. Nothing. Maybe a bird had eaten them. Maybe she'd planted them the wrong way and they were growing upside down, searching for the sun. She had to know. She stuck her finger in the dirt and felt around for the seeds.

"Wangari? What are you doing?" Maitū stood above her, a basket of greens balanced on her hip.

"I just wanted to see if it'd started growing yet."

"You have given your seeds everything they need to grow, my love—now you have to let them do it themselves. Come. Help me gather the peas."

Wangari always enjoyed helping her mother in her garden. A light rain began to fall, and she welcomed the cool drops on her skin as she knelt next to Wanjirū and snapped big peapods off their stalks. She loved everything about the garden: the birds and butterflies that came when the plants were in bloom; the variety of colors and smells; the songs her mother sang as they worked together. She reached her fingers into the soil and scooped up a handful. It felt as alive as the plants that grew in it.

She was still playing with her hands in the dirt when—*pow!*—a soft ball of damp earth landed against her shoulder.

Her older brother was home! "Nderitu!" Wangari cried, waving joyously.

Wangari was now eight years old, and Nderitu was thirteen. He was tall like their father, who was away working on a farm, and he had their mother's kind smile. Nderitu went to boarding school in the town nearby, as many of the boys in their village did.

Girls didn't usually go to school—school cost money, and families needed their daughters at home to help with chores. But Wangari loved looking through Nderitu's books, even if she couldn't read any of the words. And unlike most of the older boys, who pretended they were too big to play with younger kids, Nderitu never complained when Wangari tagged along.

"Go on," her mother said. "Playing in the rain will make you grow tall and strong, just like the plants."

Laughing, Wangari and Nderitu ran down the path together, their bare feet beating against the packed earth. The trail led to the top of a steep hill overlooking a valley. When it rained, the hill was slick with mud—perfect for Wangari's favorite game.

She took a running start and slid down the hill in a seated position, shrieking as the world sped past. She tumbled to a muddy stop at the bottom, with Nderitu close behind.

"Do you have hills like this at school?" Wangari asked when they'd both stopped laughing.

"No," Nderitu said. "I don't even want to think about what my teachers would do if I came to class with muddy trousers! Besides, I have to study—there's no time to play."

Wangari sighed. "I wish I could go, too."

They lay in the mud for a while, looking up at the cloudy sky.

"I feel sorry for you," Nderitu said after a while.

"Why?"

"Because you're not as fast as me!" And with

that he took off back up the hill, Wangari laughing and chasing behind.

~

A few nights later, Nderitu put down his bowl in the middle of dinner and said, "How come Wangari doesn't go to school?"

Wangari froze, a piece of potato halfway to her lips. Wangari looked to her mother, waiting for her to tell Nderitu to stop teasing and eat his dinner. To her surprise, Maitū appeared to be thinking it over.

"That's a good question," she said. Then she went back to her dinner as though nothing had happened.

That night, Wangari lay awake thinking about that strange conversation. A few girls in the village went to school, but not many. It was silly of Nderitu even to have asked.

Wasn't it?

~

When she came back from collecting firewood the next day, the house was unexpectedly full. Her mother was there, and so was her grandfather. Her mother's eldest brother, who they always consulted on important family decisions, was there, too. Wangari had the feeling they'd been talking about her.

"Wangari," her mother said, "we have made a decision. Your sisters are getting old enough to help me in the house. When the weather turns colder, you will be going to primary school."

Wangari sat back. School! She was going to go to school! She looked over at Nderitu, who was munching a handful of berries and seemed not to be listening to the conversation. She caught his eye and thought she saw him wink.

CHAPTER THREE

Wangari picked up her slate and eraser and placed them at the bottom of a wooden box her mother had brought home from the market. Wangari smiled when she thought about the first time she had used an eraser at Ihithe Primary School— how she'd nearly jumped from her seat as the marks disappeared from the slate like magic.

That had been nearly three years ago. Wangari was eleven now, and an even bigger adventure lay ahead. She was going to St. Cecilia's Intermediate Primary School in Nyeri, a boarding school run by Catholic nuns from Italy.

Wangari had never spent a night away from her

mother in her life, and now she was going to live in another town completely, in a dormitory with many other girls. She was leaving her garden, her village, her tree by the stream. Did they even have trees at St. Cecilia's?

"Wangari?"

She turned to see Nderitu. He, too, was going back to boarding school the next morning, to a boys' high school in the same town. Wangari tried to take comfort in the fact that he would be close by, even if they wouldn't be allowed to visit each other.

Nderitu held out a small parcel wrapped in newspaper. When Wangari tore off the paper, it turned out to be a dress just her size, in the same olive-green cloth as Nderitu's school uniform.

"I saved some money to buy fabric for new school trousers. And I bought a bit extra and had this made for you. I hope it'll fit; I didn't really—"

But before he could finish, Wangari threw her arms around him.

She squeezed her eyes shut tight to keep any tears from falling out.

~

At sunrise the next morning, Wangari got up and splashed cold water on her face. She lifted the box that contained all her belongings and slung it onto her back. Together, she, her mother, and Nderitu walked to the edge of the village. The siblings would make the four-hour walk to Nyeri alone. She would have to say goodbye to Maitū here.

Wangari had so much to say, yet no words would come out. How could she leave her mother if she didn't know how to say goodbye?

Wanjirū lifted a gentle hand and placed it on Wangari's forehead in blessing. Wangari closed her eyes and relaxed into the warm, familiar touch. She didn't have to say anything. Her mother understood. Nderitu and Wangari did not speak for the first part of the journey. Wangari was afraid she'd cry if she opened her mouth. After an hour or so, they came to the widest river Wangari had ever seen. A wooden path stretched over the rushing water, like a road floating in the air.

Wangari's feet stayed rooted where she stood. She'd never seen a bridge before.

"It's all right," her brother said. "It will hold you."

If she turned back now, she'd be home in time to collect firewood and could sit with her mother by the fire as if nothing had ever happened.

But the rest of her life was just across that river.

Wangari took a deep breath, kept her eyes straight ahead, and crossed to the other side.

~

The next day, Wangari sat in her new olive-green dress at a desk, looking out the window as she wondered what her mother and younger siblings were doing back in Ihithe. She felt a small twist in her heart.

With a heavy *thump*, the teacher placed a textbook down in front of her, bringing her attention back to the classroom. When the nun's back was turned, Wangari's curiosity and excitement overtook her. She opened the cover of the book and breathed in the smell of the pages.

She flipped through until her eyes caught on a diagram that showed little arrows connecting a series of drawings in the shape of a circle. At the top of the circle was a cluster of small, round eggs. Wangari's eyes followed the arrow as it moved from the eggs to a tadpole, then to a larger tadpole with a tail and legs, then to a full-grown frog, and finally back to the eggs.

Eggs. Tadpole. Little frog. Big frog.

This was the story of her stream! The frogs she'd seen in one season had come from the tadpoles before that, and the eggs she saw came before them. They didn't just appear and disappear at random. They were all part of the same life cycle, just like the babies, young children, parents, and old people in her village. Seeing the frog in her book now was like seeing an old friend. Ihithe didn't feel so far away anymore.

CHAPTER FOUR

J ust as tadpoles turn into frogs, Wangari grew up, too. In 1956, when she was sixteen years old, she finished St. Cecilia's with the best grades in her class and received a wonderful prize—a scholarship to Loreto Girls' High School, just outside Nairobi.

Nairobi, the capital of Kenya, was often called "the Green City in the Sun." At first, Wangari saw the city's big buildings and decided that nickname must have been chosen by someone who had never seen a place like Ihithe. It wasn't until a class trip to the Karura Forest, a cool, quiet place of towering bamboo trees just beyond the busy city center, that she understood where the name came from.

Wangari's science teacher, Mother Teresia, led the class briskly down the trail, pointing out the forest's different trees and snapping at stragglers to hurry up. Wangari walked arm in arm with her friend Makena, who grew up in the city and didn't share her passion for science and nature. "The trees all look the same to me!" she whispered behind Mother Teresia's back, which made both girls giggle. "I saw a café back near the bus. Is it lunchtime yet?"

Wangari laughed. Makena may not have been much of an outdoor person, but her instinct for finding snacks was as sharp as a lion's.

~

One afternoon, halfway through Wangari's final year at high school, she knocked on the door of a classroom she'd come to know very well.

"Mother Teresia?"

The nun looked up from a Bunsen burner, a

pair of enormous safety goggles half covering a small face framed by a broad white habit.

"Wangari!" her teacher said with delight. "Do come in. I was just preparing tomorrow's lesson. I've a basin full of beakers and test tubes to wash. I assume you don't mind if we clean while we chat?"

"Of course, Mother," Wangari said, dropping her bag and heading to the sink. Of all the teachers at Loreto, she liked Mother Teresia best. She was smart, funny, feisty, and unendingly patient. Wangari had spent many free periods in the science teacher's classroom, helping clean lab equipment and talking with Mother Teresia about science, chemistry, and biology. Wangari had always loved the natural world. Mother Teresia helped her understand the beauty the naked eye couldn't see. She had taught Wangari that chemical equations and the elements on the periodic table weren't just drawings on a page. They were the building blocks of life—from the smallest tadpole to the tallest tree.

"Have you given any more thought to your plans after graduation?"

"It depends on how I do on my exams," Wangari said, rubbing a cleaning cloth along the rim of a glass beaker.

"We both know you will do well."

"I'll do my best," Wangari said. "And if I succeed…" Wangari took a deep breath, as if about to confess a secret. "Mother Teresia, I want to go to university. Makerere University in Uganda. It's the only one in East Africa."

Not many girls in Kenya even finished high school. To dream of university felt so bold. Mother Teresia, though, seem unfazed.

"Yes, you must. With a mind like yours, there is no question about that," Mother Teresia said. "The question is: would you consider going a bit farther?"

She went to her desk and opened a folder. "The United States government is offering college

scholarships to students in Africa. We have been asked to nominate our best graduates. I think you should apply."

"America!" Wangari said, flipping through the papers. "I've never been farther than Nairobi."

"Well, then—this would be quite the adventure, wouldn't it?" Mother Teresia said. "The world is changing, Wangari. Why not change with it?"

CHAPTER FIVE

From the window of the plane, Wangari looked down at a golden expanse so large that it never seemed to end. She had read about the Sahara Desert, of course, but nothing prepared her for the sight of it from the sky.

The journey would take days: Kenya to Libya to Luxembourg to Iceland to Canada to New York City. And then, at last (Wangari checked her itinerary again, though she practically knew it by heart), to Atchison, Kansas, a little dot squarely in the middle of America.

Wangari had been thrilled to get her acceptance letter, and even happier to find that Makena was accepted to the same all-women's university: Mount St. Scholastica. Wangari looked down fondly at her friend, who snored in the seat next to her with her head on Wangari's shoulder. Makena was drooling. Wangari left her friend to sleep and turned her attention back to the window.

The plane rumbled across the sky toward a sun that never seemed to set. She thought back to the first time she had left home with Nderitu, how even walking the small footbridge outside their village had seemed like crossing the sea. And now here she was, twenty years old, with the whole ocean ahead of her.

~

In New York, Wangari, Makena, and the other Kenyan students boarded a Greyhound bus that would take them to their universities. Wangari marveled at mile upon mile of corn along the highway, enough to feed every person in Ihithe for years. By the time they reached Indiana, everyone on the bus was tired, hungry, and ready for a break.

"Cold drinks!" Makena shouted, pointing to a highway sign. Wangari sighed in relief— Makena's talent for finding snacks apparently worked anywhere in the world.

They tumbled from the bus, grateful for the fresh air and the chance to stretch their legs. The café wasn't that crowded, but Wangari noticed some strange looks from the seated customers. *They must be tired from their travels*, she thought.

"Ahem," said a voice. They turned around to face a man in a white paper server's cap.

"I have to ask you to leave," he said, his eyes never quite meeting her own. "If you're thirsty, you can buy a drink up front. You just have to drink it outside."

"Why?" Makena asked in confusion.

"We don't serve your kind here."

Wangari felt like she'd been struck. She could not believe what she was hearing. Suddenly, she realized that all the faces in the café were white.

The customers nearby fell silent.

"What should we do, Wangari?" Makena whispered.

Wangari could feel her friends looking to her for an answer. She had never been in a situation like this. At school and at home, she had been raised to follow the rules. But she also knew that some rules should be broken.

"We have no use for a place that will not treat us as equals," Wangari said, her voice sure and strong. She turned around, and her friends went with her. They walked out with their heads held high.

The bus was quiet after that. Wangari suspected the others were as shaken as she was.

Growing up in Kenya, Wangari had seen how towns and cities were divided into separate areas based on people's skin color. White children and black children didn't go to school together. Even the nuns at St. Cecilia's ran a separate school that only white girls were allowed to attend. They never talked in school about whether this was fair or not. It was just the way it was.

The white people who moved to Kenya often lived in big houses on the best land. The neighborhoods reserved for black people were crowded and farther from roads or water. White farmers were allowed to own land, chop down any trees they wanted, and grow crops that could be sold for lots of money, like tea and coffee. Black farmers had no choice but to work on white people's farms. Wangari's own father worked on a British settler's farm, one far away from Ihithe. It was the only way he could earn enough to support their family. She hardly ever saw him.

Yet Wangari could not remember a time when she felt prejudice directed at her as it was in that diner. People had warned her that there were places in America where she would not be welcome, but she hadn't really believed it. This was 1960. America called itself "the land of the free." It had the fastest cars and the highest buildings. How could it be so backward in its thinking about the color of people's skin?

By the time she and Makena arrived in Atchison, her worry had hardened into a knot in her stomach. A dark-haired young woman with white skin noticed them and walked quickly in their direction. Wangari took a deep breath and stood as tall as she could.

The young woman smiled broadly and held out her hand. "Wangari? Makena? What a pleasure to meet you. I'm Florence. Welcome to Mount St. Scholastica!"

Wangari relaxed, and she reached out to shake hands with her first American friend.

~

Wangari made a lot of wonderful memories with her friends in America. Kenya was too far away for her to travel home during school breaks, so Wangari spent holidays and long weekends with Florence at her family's house where they baked chocolate chip cookies, danced along with *American Bandstand* on television, and stayed up late laughing and talking.

She also loved watching the seasons change. In the springtime Wangari left early for classes so she could walk slowly and admire the latest buds and seedlings sprouting from the naked branches and damp earth. Wangari majored, of course, in biology—the study of living things. Over the summer breaks, she worked at laboratories to get the skills she'd need to become a scientist.

There was a lot to learn outside the lab, too.

America was changing all around her. Black people were tired of the kind of discrimination Wangari and her friends experienced when

they first arrived. To fight it, they sometimes refused to go to businesses that treated black and white customers differently. In other cases, hundreds or even thousands of people marched through American cities together to protest unfair treatment. Sometimes people screamed nasty things at them. Sometimes they were even arrested and thrown in jail.

But they never gave up. Wangari was amazed by the marchers' courage.

Wangari often thought about her home. *Why do white people in Kenya have more say over the land than black people? Why is it all right for British settlers to decide to cut down trees that have stood for centuries?* Kenya was a British colony—a part of the world Britain controlled as if it was part of their own country, no matter how far away it was. There had been ugly fights between the British and the Kenyans who wanted to rebel against their control. She tried to imagine the streets of Nairobi filled with people marching together, but she couldn't. It was exciting to see people in America speaking up about the problems in their country now—and trying to fix them.

She was startled from her thoughts by pounding on her apartment door. "Open up, Wangari!" a familiar voice cried out. As soon as she did, a breathless Makena came in.

"I have been looking everywhere for you!" Makena paused to catch her breath. "We have news. From home. Kenya is going to be independent. Look!" Makena smoothed a folded newspaper onto the kitchen table. "My eldest sister sent this to me, special delivery. There will be elections in May for the new leaders who will take over when the British leave. By the end of the year, Kenya will be its own country!"

Wangari looked at the newspaper, stunned. For as long as she'd been alive, Kenya had belonged to Britain. Now it would be its own country. For the first time, Kenyans would decide for themselves how to run their country. Kenyans would have the right to decide what was fair and what wasn't, to protect their land and rights, just as she saw people in America doing.

Wangari wanted to see this new country right away, but there was also more she wanted to learn. She had already agreed to attend the University of Pittsburgh after she graduated from Mount St. Scholastica. As she and Makena hugged each other, Wangari knew that one day she *would* return home to a free Kenya. She was excited to see what that would mean.

CHAPTER SIX

As soon as she stepped off the plane in Nairobi, Wangari felt at home. The warm, dry air that wrapped around her like a hug was nothing like the snow she'd left behind in Pennsylvania. It had been six years since she'd set foot in Kenya, and the city seemed to buzz with more people, more energy, and more excitement than she remembered.

"Wangari!" cried a tall young man with a familiar face. Instantly Wangari saw the people behind him, all waving and leaping with joy: her mother, her siblings—even her father had come out from the farm.

"Nderitu!" she said, throwing her arms around

her brother. "Look at you!"

He laughed. "Don't you recognize your baby brother? I'm Kamunya. That's Nderitu!" he said. Their elder brother approached, laughing, holding the hand of a smiling young woman. Wangari recognized her from the photographs he'd sent of his wife, Elizabeth.

"How on earth did you grow this tall?" Wangari said to her brothers. "What else has changed while I was gone?"

Nderitu put his arm around her shoulders. "Everything, sis. Now hand me those bags."

~

Wangari didn't have to worry about finding a place to live. Nderitu and Elizabeth invited her to stay with them in their small house in Nairobi. She didn't have to worry about finding work, either. The University of Nairobi was looking for a person with exactly the skills she'd picked up at her summer jobs. She could work there as a teacher and research assistant while also taking classes for her doctorate degree.

But not everything went smoothly. Her male students didn't believe that a woman, especially one as young as Wangari, could teach them anything. Wangari thought about the best teachers she'd ever had—including Mother Teresia and her mother. They had always spoken to her one-on-one. So that's what Wangari decided to do with her students. As they worked through the lab exercises, she walked around the room, pausing to guide them through any problems. People were more willing to listen if you took the time to connect with them, she found, rather than just telling them what to do. She might look different from the teachers they were used to, Wangari told herself, but her students would get used to it. This was a new Kenya.

Life at home was different, too. In 1969, she married a man named Mwangi Mathai. He was a good husband—quiet and serious, and he worked in politics. They lived in Nairobi and soon had a son, Waweru, a daughter, Wanjira, and then another son, Muta. Mwangi sometimes got annoyed when Wangari worked late instead of hosting dinners like other politicians' wives, but Wangari didn't let it bother her too much.

In 1971, after years of studying, Wangari got her doctorate degree—the first woman in East or Central Africa to do so. Wangari was pregnant with Wanjira when she put on a long black robe and squishy cap and walked across the stage to receive her diploma.

She was Dr. Wangari Mathai now.

~

Not all the changes happening in Kenya were good ones. Wangari looked eagerly out the car window as they bumped along the dusty road from Nairobi to Ihithe. It was 1973 and she hadn't been to the village in years. She couldn't wait to see it again.

"Are you certain we're going the right way?" she asked the driver.

This didn't look like the road to her village. There were broad, dusty patches where groves of tall trees had once stood; they had been torn away to make room for coffee plantations. The stream running along the road, which used to be clear and clean, was a river of mud.

Soil erosion, Wangari thought. Tree roots hold soil in place. Whoever had cut down the trees hadn't realized that. Now the rivers that used to provide fresh water were impossible to drink from.

The car pulled into Ihithe, and Wangari's face fell. The same mud-walled houses stood in the same places, but everything else was wrong. The cows outside the houses were so skinny she could count their ribs. The sun beat down on dry earth that was stripped of grass and bushes. Even the people looked thinner.

She found her mother outside her hut mending a basket.

Wanjirū looked up. She was happy to see her daughter, but her eyes were lined with sorrow. She saw the worry in Wangari's face as well.

"Come," she said. "It's worse than you think."

They walked down the hill where Wangari and her siblings had once gone mud-skiing.

"Children can't play here during the rainy season anymore," Maitū explained. "There have been too many landslides."

When they reached the top of the valley, Wangari gasped. The land where the forest used to be was now bare, cracked, and brown.

"They cut it down," Maitū said with a soft sigh. "Farmers thought they'd make more money if they grew tea and coffee to sell. The truth is, it's made us all poorer. We have to walk so far to find firewood and clean water."

Wangari knelt down and scooped up a handful of dirt. It was nothing like the rich earth she'd touched as a child.

Maitū continued. "The crops don't grow as well as they used to, and most of the old fruit trees are gone. The money from the crops doesn't come to us, either. It goes to people who are rich already. And instead of eating what we grow, we have to buy food at the market."

When they came to the bottom of the hill, Wangari stopped in her tracks. Her eyes filled with tears. The mugumo, her wild fig tree, was gone. The arrowroots and the stream were gone, too. Where the tree had once stood was a patch of empty dirt.

"A big man bought this piece of land," Maitū said sadly. "He thought he'd make a lot of money by planting tea trees. He said the fig tree would

just be in the way, so he cut it down. But once the tree was gone, the stream dried up. Now nothing can grow here. That man killed our tree for nothing." Her voice sounded bitter. "People stopped listening. They stopped respecting the land. And now we're all paying for it."

~

Wangari did not go straight back to Nairobi. Instead, she directed the driver to other rural villages, places where her school friends and cousins lived. The story was the same everywhere. Healthy trees and grassland had been replaced by non-native trees that didn't hold the soil. Rivers were muddy. Dust blew all over.

Wangari knew something had to be done.

CHAPTER SEVEN

W angari was part of a group called
the National Council of Women
of Kenya—NCWK for short. It
was made up of women across the country who
wanted to help Kenya and their communities. She
knew that if any group of people could figure out
how to fix the problems in the countryside, this
would be the one.

One Saturday, they squeezed into the tiny
office that housed their many projects. A tower
of papers began to topple, but Wangari caught
it just before it fell. Another woman looked for
a place to put a stack of books. Finding none, she
set them in her lap with a sigh.

Wangari described what she had seen in Ihithe. Most had heard similar things from relatives around the country.

"We have to do something," a woman named Vertistine said with a decisive nod.

Vertistine was also a science professor at the University of Nairobi and one of Wangari's closest friends. She went by the nickname Vert. She was a black American woman who had moved to Nairobi with her Kenyan husband, and she spoke in an honest way that Wangari liked.

"I always ask my students, 'What's the problem you're trying to solve?'" Vert said. "Let's do that here. What's the real problem facing these communities?"

"Is it that they don't have enough money?" someone said.

"The villages have always been poor, but never like this," said another woman.

"Should we donate food?"

"No, we should raise money."

While the women debated, Wangari's mind was working. The people and animals were sick because they didn't have enough food. They didn't have enough food because the land was not healthy, and the land had gone bad because the streams had dried up. And all that had started when they chopped down the trees.

"Trees!" she said suddenly. The other women looked at her, startled and a bit confused.

"Wangari?" Vert said. "Are you all right?"

Wangari stood up and raced to a blackboard in the corner. She drew a diagram like the one she remembered from her childhood textbook, but with arrows pointing to the center instead of around in a circle.

"Every problem comes back to one thing," she said, scribbling furiously. "The women need firewood to cook. They need food for their cattle and goats. They need shade, and fresh fruits, and healthy streams and soil to grow their crops. And what provides all that?" She put down the chalk and stepped away from the board. In the center of her notes she had drawn a giant tree.

The room was quiet.

"Who's going to go around planting all these trees?" a woman asked, folding her arms across her chest.

"We will," Wangari said. "The women of Kenya. We'll teach other women how to do it. Who knows this land better than the women who have been living on it for generations?"

"We could even pay them for every tree they keep alive, help them earn a bit of money for their families," Vert said. Wangari smiled. Her friend got it. She always did.

Some of the women still looked doubtful. That was all right. It took people a while to get used to something new. The woman with the crossed arms gave her a tough look. "You really think planting trees is going to make a difference?" she asked.

Wangari looked out the window. A hummingbird was hovering outside, its tiny wings beating tirelessly.

"I don't know," she said. "But we have to try."

~

As an instructor, Wangari knew that before you could teach someone how to do something, you had to do it yourself. With that in mind, she organized a big party to show people in Nairobi how easy it was to plant a tree. She had the perfect day for it: June 5, 1977, World Environment Day.

On the day of the event, Nairobi's Kamukunji Park was crowded with families, students, and government officials. In her bright, patterned dress, Wangari looked as joyful as a flower bed. Lined up on the ground were the day's guests of honor: seven young potted trees, each honoring a community leader from a different ethnic group in Kenya.

Wangari and six others picked up shovels, and cheers and whoops rose from the crowd. As Wangari plunged her shovel into the earth, she remembered tending her garden in Ihithe, and she felt once again the joy of working with the land.

When the holes were dug, Wangari and the others carefully lifted the young trees from their pots and placed them into the soil. The trees were shorter than she was. Wangari hoped that by the time the kids running through the crowd were old enough to bring their own children here, the trees would be tall enough that their canopies would touch one another, like a green belt across the sky.

The Green Belt Movement! That is the perfect name for our project, she thought.

But even as she admired their work, she felt an uncomfortable presence behind her. She turned

around to face a sour-looking man in a suit.

This was Daniel arap Moi, the vice president of Kenya. The NCWK had invited several important people from the government to the party, and many of them came. Only Moi looked unhappy to be there. His face made clear that he did not think much of trees—or of this celebration.

"I thought you were an educated woman, Dr. Mathai," he sneered. "Why are you working the earth like a common farmer?"

"I thought *you* were an educated man, Vice President," she replied. "How can an educated person not recognize how precious this earth is?"

His face turned hard and cold before he walked away. Wangari had a bad feeling that they would meet again.

CHAPTER EIGHT

Wangari carefully patted the soil around a little green seedling. "Now you just give it some water..." she said to the group of women before her. "There! When you're all done planting, it will look like this." She sat back and gestured proudly at the seedling. She'd come to this village straight from the university, and dirt now stained the skirt of her long blue dress.

"What if it doesn't grow?" a worried-looking woman said.

Wangari's favorite students at the university were also the ones who asked lots of questions.

"Madam, what is your name?" Wangari asked.

"Grace," the woman said.

"Have you ever grown anything before, Grace?"

"Oh, many crops," Grace said. "Arrowroot, potatoes, greens…"

"And did they grow well?"

Grace nodded.

"Then do what you did then. Use your woman sense. When it looks dry, give it water. If pests attack, drive them off. And if you need help,

someone from our organization will come," she said. "All I am asking is that you try."

~

Wangari and the other Green Belt Movement volunteers bought almost every seedling in Nairobi. With nowhere else to put them, Wangari volunteered her home. It looked like a tiny forest was threatening to swallow the house.

Her children loved it. Waweru and Wanjira chased each other through the plants. The youngest boy, Muta, could often be found crawling among the tiny trees, just as Wangari used to curl up under the arrowroots.

"It's not that I don't like trees," Mwangi said. "But do they all have to be in our house?"

"It's only temporary," Wangari said. "I need to put them somewhere before we take them to the villages for planting."

"But they're everywhere!" Mwangi grumbled. "I can barely make it out my own front gate. And...good Lord, what did I just trip on?"

He reached down into a dense patch of green and felt around. He came back up with a blinking, surprised-looking Muta covered in leaves and dirt. Mwangi shot Wangari a warning look. "I want them out of our house. *Now.*"

"Okay, okay," she said, holding up her hands. "I'll see what I can do."

~

That wasn't the only reason the trees couldn't stay. Travel was difficult on a seedling, and many died on the trip from Nairobi to the countryside before they could be planted. It would be better if women cared for the young trees close to their homes. All they needed were seeds.

There was just one problem: no one would sell them any seeds.

Wangari stood before a forester behind a big desk. She waved her order for several thousand trees, but he seemed unmoved.

"We can pay for them. Why on earth won't you sell to me?"

"Women have no business planting trees," he said. "It requires *science*. Men go to university for years to become professional foresters. And you think you can just hand some seeds to women who can't even read and suddenly there will be new forests across Kenya?" He waved his hand and laughed at the idea.

Nonsense, Wangari thought. Tree planting is simple: dig a hole, put a tree in, water it, and care for it. Even women who had never gone to school could do those things.

Wangari thought of her mother tending a newly sprouted plant and of the way she tried to protect each one. This man had clearly never seen the clever ways women worked, even without schooling. She would have to show him.

"Why don't you come with me to see how the women have raised their trees so far?" Wangari said. "If you're satisfied with the way the plants look, you give me the seeds. And if you aren't, I'll never bother you again."

~

Wangari and the forester pulled up to a village outside Nairobi. As they got out of the car, a woman came hurrying down the path toward them.

"Dr. Mathai!" Grace called. "We have so much to show you since your last visit."

Grace led Wangari and the forester past dozens of young trees that looked as strong and healthy as those in any Nairobi nursery. Women in bright-colored headscarves were tending the shoots and plucking away weeds.

The forester reached out to touch one of the young plants. A woman smacked his hand away. He pulled it back sheepishly.

"At first it was difficult," Grace said, showing them into a mud hut lined with shelves of seedlings in clay pots. "The goats were eating our seedlings before they could even grow. So we put our youngest trees here."

"You have no irrigation. How do you water them?" the forester sputtered.

"Like this," Grace said. She picked up a tin can and dipped it into a waiting bucket. Water poured from holes punched in the bottom, like a watering can.

The forester didn't say a word during the drive back to Nairobi. When they arrived, before they went their separate ways, he paused.

"Come back to my office tomorrow," he said without looking at Wangari. "You can have your seeds."

Wangari waited until the car had pulled away to clap her hands with joy.

~

It was late when she got home. She closed the door quietly, expecting everyone to be asleep. She was surprised to see Mwangi sitting in the living room. He looked annoyed.

"Where have you been?" he said. "It's late."

"I'm sorry, it was a long day—but such a good one! We got the seeds we needed…"

"You spend too much time on those trees," he

complained. "You have a family at home. You are married to a politician. Why are you doing things for these women all the time? They can't vote for me. They can't pay you."

"I promised to help them," Wangari said.

"That doesn't mean you have to."

"Is that so?" Wangari said, growing angry. "Is that how you feel about the men who voted for you because you said you'd help them find jobs?"

"That's none of your business!" Mwangi snapped. With that, he marched off to bed.

~

The next night, Wangari got home late again. The children were asleep in their beds. She stepped into her bedroom quietly, but something was different. The gentle snoring she always heard at this time of night was gone.

She switched on a lamp. The bed was neatly made. Mwangi wasn't there. His clothes, his books, and even his toothbrush—they weren't there either.

Mwangi had left.

Is there anything worse than losing the person you once loved? she thought. And then she realized: yes. The worst thing would be losing herself. If Mwangi did not like her choices, it was better that they go their separate ways.

She closed her eyes. In the morning, she would tell the children, and they would begin their new life. But tonight, she would get some sleep.

CHAPTER NINE

Now that Wangari and Mwangi weren't married, it didn't seem right to still have his last name. At the same time, Wangari didn't want to give up the name that she shared with her children and that reminded her of the happy times they'd had as a family. She decided to keep the name, but make it her own.

A Kikuyu person pronouncing "Mathai" would say it like this: "Ma'athai." If she spelled her last name with two *a*'s instead of just one, Wangari could create a name that honored all the different parts of her life—and belonged to her alone. Now she would be known as Dr. Wangari Maathai.

She made one other big decision, too: she was

going to run for election. She wanted to become a member of Parliament and have a say in Kenya's government. According to election rules, she'd have to quit her job as a university professor. It would be worth it, she told herself, if she had a voice in the laws that affected people's lives.

~

Late one night, after they'd both finished marking papers at the university, Wangari and Vert sat in the NCWK offices looking over letters from communities around the country asking to be part of the tree-planting movement.

"There are so many!" Vert said as she flipped through the pile.

Wangari was happy to see how much people cared about their environment. But she was also worried for Kenya's future. The old president had died, and the new president was Moi, the unpleasant man she'd met at Kamukunji Park.

Since Moi became president, the government officials were less helpful to her and to her fellow Green Belt Movement volunteers. She thought she knew why. Whenever she met someone who wanted to plant trees, Wangari asked them where they thought the problems with their land had started. And the answer was always the same: the government.

The government sold away public land that used to belong to everyone. The government cut down the national forests for money.

It wasn't right. So along with planting trees, Wangari started teaching people how to stand up for their communities. She explained that if the government wasn't making sure that villages had clean water or was ruining the environment by chopping down trees, people had a right to speak up. They could write letters to newspapers or elected officials, or they could organize protest marches. That was how a free country worked.

Wangari felt like she wasn't planting just trees anymore. She was planting ideas, too.

"We wanted Kenya to be free," Vert said, taking off her glasses and rubbing her eyes. "What good is independence if the new rulers are going to destroy the land just like the old ones did?"

"We need people in government who want to lead. Not just rule," Wangari said. She felt even more sure about her decision to run for Parliament.

~

A few weeks later, Wangari was asked to report to the board of elections. She knocked on the door of the Nairobi office.

"Dr. Maathai," the head of the election board said. He was grinning in a way Wangari did not like at all. "I'm sorry to have you come so far just to get bad news, but—you cannot run for Parliament. You must end your candidacy right away."

Wangari felt her blood run cold. "Why?"

"We've looked at your old voting registration records. And it seems that you forgot to check a box on your form back in...let's see...1979."

"That's silly! That's a mistake, not a crime."

The man shrugged. "Rules are rules."

"Are they? The rules don't seem to count when President Moi's government is selling away the land."

At that his smile disappeared. They stared at each other across the desk. Wangari was furious, but she knew she would not win this battle. With any luck, it would not be too late to get her job at the university back. She stood up to leave.

"Oh, and, Dr. Maathai," the man said, his evil grin returning. "Don't bother calling the university. Your position has been filled already. President Moi made sure of that."

~

Wangari walked the streets in a daze. She was not allowed to run for Parliament. She had lost her job. She was even going to lose her home—the house belonged to the university. If she didn't work there anymore, she couldn't live there, either. She dreaded telling her kids.

She wanted to cry, to shout, but there was no one to hear. She took a deep breath. Wangari

never liked to dwell too long on troubles. No matter how bad things got, there was always some way forward, even if it took a while to find. In the meantime, she'd keep working at the Green Belt Movement.

As she opened the office door, she half hoped no one would be there. Instead, she entered a room full of cheering, celebrating employees and volunteers.

Vert swept in and grabbed her by the shoulders.

"Wangari! It's fantastic. Have you seen this?" she said, shaking a paper in front of her.

Wangari looked at the name at the top of the letter: the United Nations Voluntary Fund for the Decade of Women.

The organizers had heard about the Green Belt Movement. They wanted to give them some money. A lot of money, actually—enough to keep the Green Belt Movement running for years.

Wangari became the full-time director of the Green Belt Movement. Women planted trees in rows a thousand trees long, truly creating the green belt she had imagined.

But she was about to confront her biggest challenge yet—right in her own backyard.

CHAPTER TEN

I t was late at night when the knock came on Wangari's office door.

She didn't recognize the young man standing there. He looked frightened, and he kept looking over his shoulder as he stepped inside.

"Thank you for seeing me," he said. "I am so sorry to bother you this late. It's just—something terrible is happening, and you're the only person I could think of who might be able to help."

He rustled through his bag and pulled out a tightly folded packet from the bottom. He unfolded it onto a conference table. It was a map of Uhuru Park, one of the biggest parks in Nairobi. *Uhuru* meant "freedom," and that was what the park was meant to be—a place where all Nairobi's people could feel free and peaceful. It gave them a cool, shady place to escape from the bustle of the city and reconnect with nature, for no money at all.

But under President Moi, nothing in Kenya was truly free.

A blueprint showed plans for a huge skyscraper right in the center of the park. Inside would be Moi's main office. With at least sixty stories planned, it would cast a shadow over everything below it. A giant parking lot would also cover the green grass. There was even a spot marked for a giant statue of President Moi.

"This will ruin the park!" Wangari said. "When do they want to start?"

"Right away. These plans are supposed to be top secret, but once I saw them, I knew someone had to do something."

"You did the right thing," Wangari said.

"May I ask you just one favor? Please don't tell anyone how you found out about this."

The young man's eyes were full of fear. There were rumors that bad things happened to people just for criticizing Moi or his decisions.

This young man wasn't risking just his job or his reputation to tell her this: he was risking his life. And by agreeing to help, Wangari was now, too.

She placed a hand on his shoulder and met his gaze. "I promise."

~

Wangari started writing. She wrote a letter to the government asking them to admit to their plans to destroy Uhuru Park. When no reply came, she wrote to the United Nations. In these letters she asked for a truthful account of what the government was planning and for help stopping it. She also wrote to newspapers so that journalists could look into it, too, and could tell the people of Kenya what was happening.

"GIANT SKYSCRAPER PLANNED FOR UHURU PARK," read headlines. On the front page was a photograph of a construction fence that had been built in the park overnight.

"What should we do, Wangari?"

Since news of the park came out, Wangari was asked this question everywhere she went. She got calls at her office and letters at her home. She took a deep breath and said, "Make your voice heard." She kept her voice calm. There was no need to make anyone more afraid. "Write letters. Tell your leaders what you think. Do anything you can. Just don't be silent."

~

A few days later, on her walk to work, she spotted a familiar face. Makena was rushing by. She didn't seem to see Wangari.

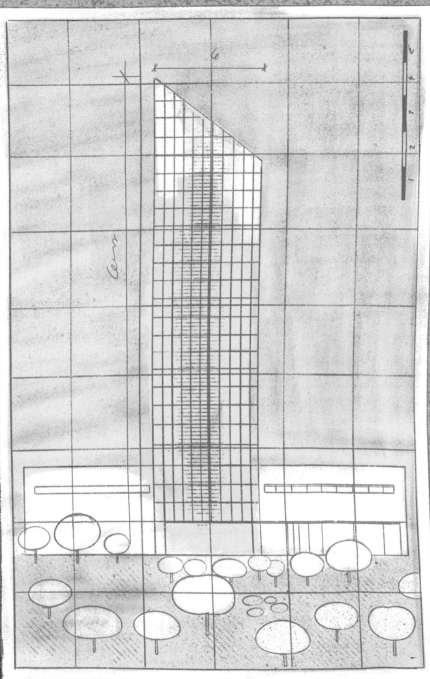

"Makena!" Wangari called. "How wonderful to see you!"

Instead of returning Wangari's greeting, her old friend seemed to edge away, as though Wangari had a virus she was afraid to catch.

"I'm sorry, Wangari," she whispered. "My husband said not to speak to you anymore. This business with the park—it's just too dangerous."

"But, Makena—we have to speak up!"

"I'd rather be silent if speaking out means risking my family's safety," she said. "I'm sorry. I have to go. Please understand." And she walked away.

Wangari's heart sank as she watched her go. Maybe this was a battle she'd have to fight alone.

She looked down at the newspaper in her hand. There was a photograph of her on the front page. "MAATHAI TELLS MOI: NOT IN OUR PARK," blared the headline. Wangari opened the paper.

Inside she saw letter after letter. They were from old people and young people, wealthy people and poor, all addressed to the government leaders who were trying to take their park away.

"Where is your sense of pride in the people you lead?" one person wrote. "Where is your pride in our beautiful country? You should be ashamed."

"We deserve our park—and we deserve to debate these matters freely, without fearing abuse from you," another wrote.

There was even a letter from a young child: "Uhuru Park is where my parents take me every weekend. Please don't tear it down."

With every page, Wangari's spirits lifted.

~

The people of Kenya had made their voices heard, but still the government wouldn't listen. President Moi had convinced powerful people in other countries to give him the money he needed to build his new office, and he wasn't backing down. So Wangari started writing letters to those people, too. She sent letters to Canada, to Germany, to the United States, and even to the United Kingdom.

"Do not let President Moi destroy Uhuru Park," she wrote. "Please do not give him any more money. He does not think about what is good for his people, but only what is good for himself.

"This park provides fresh air to the millions of people living in Nairobi and a place to play or get away from busy city life. We must protect our environment and green spaces above everything else."

Because of her letters, American and British newspapers started reporting on what was happening in Kenya. People all over the world heard Africans speaking up for themselves and asked their own governments to help. Soon, the plans for the park began to get smaller.

~

Still, the fight continued for a few more years. Neither the government nor Wangari would give up. Then, one morning in February 1992, Wangari heard the news that the construction fence had been taken down.

The park was saved!

Wangari met her friends in Uhuru Park to celebrate with a victory dance. Together, they lifted their arms and their voices to share their joy.

Like the hummingbird trying to put out a fire, it had been the small acts of individual Kenyans that saved the park. Wangari's letters inspired others to write to the newspapers about what was important to them. It was just like planting trees. When each person planted a single tree, together, they created a forest. When each person raised their voice, together, they created a movement.

AFTERWORD

The fight for Uhuru Park was not Wangari's last clash with the government. Like many activists in Kenya, she endured prison and beatings for opposing the president. But she never backed down.

When it came time to vote in 2002, the Kenyan people were fed up with President Moi. They voted his ruling party out and instead chose candidates who wanted ordinary Kenyans to have a voice.

One of those new lawmakers was Wangari. She was elected to serve as a member of Parliament in 2003 and was named assistant minister in the Ministry for Environment and Natural Resources. Having seen how much influence the government could have on people's lives, she was determined to use it to help people and the land.

In 2004, Wangari won the Nobel Peace Prize. It was the first time the prize was given to a woman from Africa, and the first time it went to an environmentalist. In her acceptance speech, Wangari told the story of the stream she had played in as a child and the frogs she used to marvel at in all their life stages.

"The challenge," she said, "is to restore the home of the tadpoles and give back to our children a world of beauty and wonder."

After winning the Nobel Prize, Wangari chose to educate as many people as she could about the environment. She planted a tree with US Senator Barack Obama, who later became president of the United States. In the 1960s, Obama's father had also traveled from Kenya to study in the US, just like Wangari.

Wangari died in Nairobi on September 25, 2011, at the age of seventy-one, due to complications from cancer. Her legacy lives on in the millions of trees she helped plant and the millions of people inspired by her work. The Green Belt Movement has planted fifty-one million trees in Kenya alone, and her children continue the work their mother began so many years ago.

Two of those seven trees planted by the first Green Belt Movement volunteers in Kamukunji Park are still alive today, and they continue to provide shade and beauty to people in Nairobi. As the hummingbird in Wangari's beloved tale shows, every effort counts.

THE POWER OF ONE

Inspired by the hummingbird in the story on pages 14-17, Wangari believed in the power of one. This is the idea that each of us, in our own small way, can make a difference. She knew that if everyone took it upon themselves to plant one tree, they would soon have a forest. She was right! Wangari passed the idea of the power of one on to her environmental organization, the Green Belt Movement, which consists of women who still work together to plant trees today.

Wangari used her power of one to help nature and to plant trees. On a separate piece of paper, list some of the things that matter to you. Is it trees, like Wangari? Maybe it's animals, or other people.

Now pick one and think about it a little harder.

- Why is this one thing important to you?

- Why might it be important to others?

- What is one small thing you can do to help?

THE GREEN JENERATION

The Green Jeneration (the *J* stands for "junior"!) is a movement created by Wangari's granddaughters, Ruth Wangari and Elsa Wanjiru, and their friends that allows children to plant flowers, trees, or vegetables in community spaces. The project understands that plants contribute to the livelihood and well-being of the community.

Spending time in nature also lets us appreciate the air we breathe, the food we eat, the water we drink, the plant medicine that heals us, and the beauty that surrounds us. Exercise your power like Wangari did by giving back to the world that gives us life.

1. Gather your materials:

- *A container for your plant, such as a recycled can, a flowerpot, a tightly woven basket, or even an old rubber boot*

- *A dish or plastic lid to catch the drainage*

- *Soil*

- *Seeds; choose whatever you'd like—flowers, herbs, or a small tree of your own!*

- *Spray bottle*

- *Plastic wrap*

2. Have an adult help you poke a few holes in the bottom of your planter, if it doesn't already have them.

3. Fill the container ¾ of the way with soil.

4. Follow the instructions on the seed packet for planting depth.

5. Place your seeds in the hole you've created.

6. Cover the hole with soil.

7. Place the container on the dish and water your seeds. Cover the container with plastic wrap to keep in the moisture.

8. Place your potted plant by a window and watch over the coming weeks as it grows! Be sure to water your plant every few days. You can check

if your plant needs water by touching the soil. If it feels dry, your plant needs water!

9. Once your seedling grows so tall that it touches the plastic wrap, remove the covering.

THE INTERCONNECTEDNESS OF LIVING THINGS

Wangari believed that all living things are interconnected, meaning they need one another to survive. When she studied a frog's life cycle at school (pages 32-34), she remembered the frog eggs she once saw in the stream by her home. Later in life, Wangari realized she needed to plant trees to protect the stream and its fresh water so creatures like the frogs would have a place to live.

Think about your favorite animal. What does it need to survive and thrive? On a separate piece of paper, draw your animal's life cycle and make a list of some things you can do to protect its home.

You can look at the image of the life cycle of a frog, shown on the facing page, to get you started.

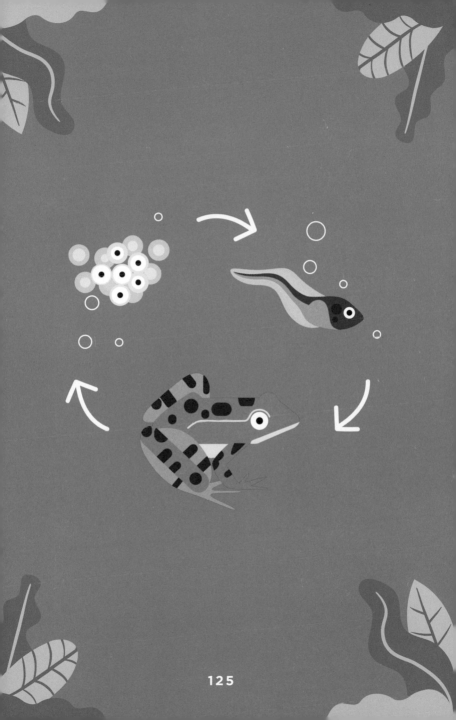

THE GREEN BELT MOVEMENT

The Green Belt Movement (GBM) is an environmental organization founded by Professor Wangari Maathai in 1977 to empower communities, particularly women, to save the environment and improve livelihoods. In response to the needs of rural Kenyan women, GBM encourages them to work together to improve the surrounding land and local economies by growing seedlings and planting trees in order to bind the soil, store rainwater, and provide food and firewood. They receive a small monetary token for their work.

THE WANGARI MAATHAI FOUNDATION

Inspired by the legacy of the 2004 Nobel Peace laureate Wangari Maathai, the Wangari Maathai Foundation is a nonprofit dedicated to inspiring courageous and responsible leadership in youth and children. The Foundation uses the idea of the power of one to nurture a culture of integrity, purpose, and personal responsibility that will transform the future. The Green Jeneration is one of the Foundation's many youth initiatives.

ACKNOWLEDGMENTS

Dr. Wangari Maathai proved that women can move the earth (literally) when presented with the right leadership, tools, and mission.

Corinne, your writing leaves an everlasting mark. You've crafted Dr. Maathai's legacy so that young minds might learn the enormous impact that one woman's efforts can have on the world. Eugenia Mello, thank you for your energy and passion from the start. You've handled the challenge of illustrating Dr. Maathai's life with respect and a deft hand. Thank you, too, to Martha Cipolla and Marisa Finkelstein for your thoughtful reads.

Wanjira Mathai was so very helpful in realizing our dreams for this book's impact. Thank you for being so open to collaboration—and for the work you do to expand your mother's mission every day.

And finally, Rebel Girls would like to thank our readers. Your continued interest drives the mission further than we'd ever dreamed. Remember the hummingbird. Even one small effort—an act of courage—can inspire big change.

ABOUT REBEL GIRLS

Rebel Girls is an award-winning cultural media engine founded in 2012, spanning over seventy countries. Through a combination of thought-provoking stories, creative expression, and business innovation, Rebel Girls is on a mission to balance power and create a more inclusive world. Rebel Girls is home to a diverse and passionate group of rebels who work in Los Angeles, New York, Atlanta, Merida (Mexico), London, and Milan.

Find Rebel Girls online (rebelgirls.co), on Facebook (Facebook.com/rebelgirls), Instagram (@rebelgirls), and Twitter (@rebelgirlsbook).